The Dawn Fairy

by Keith Faulkner

illustrated by Helen Cann

Cartwheel BOOKS®

SCHOLASTIC INC.

New York Toronto London Auckland Sydney
Mexico City New Delhi Hong Kong

The sun was just rising and the birds were beginning to sing, but the Dawn Fairy was already up and busy. Every morning she collected the sparkling drops of dew from the flowers to make into fairy juice.

She heard the sound of a child's laughter, and as the child ran by she saw something sparkling fall to the ground. It was a tiny silver fairy necklace.

"I must keep it safe," said the fairy, "until I find a way to give it back."

The Dawn Fairy looked for a place to hide the necklace, where it would be safe. She tried a hole in a nearby tree, hiding the sparkling necklace deep in the darkness. As she was leaving, she saw some squirrels scampering around in the branches.

"The squirrels are sure to find the necklace," the fairy whispered to herself as she saw them getting closer to the hole. So with a flutter of her shining wings, she flew back to get it.

Looking around, she saw some flowers with big bell-shaped
blossoms and hid the necklace inside one of them. Then she
waited and watched to see if the necklace was safe.

BZZZ...BZZZ...BZZZ. A big bumblebee came flying along,
stopping at each of the flowers to sip the nectar.
"It's sure to find the necklace," gasped the fairy, and although she
was hardly bigger than the bee herself, she chased it away
and got the necklace back again.

Still trying to find a safe place to hide the necklace,
the Dawn Fairy flew down to the pond.
"I'm sure it will be safe hidden in the reeds," she said to herself, but
just then she saw the beady eyes of a frog watching her from the water.

The sun was going down, but the Dawn Fairy still hadn't found
a safe place to hide the sparkling necklace. She flew back to her
home deep inside the wild rosebush. Then she placed her head on
a rosebud, and clasping the necklace, she went to sleep—
her body floating in the air, light as thistledown.

In the early morning, as the first bird began to sing, the Dawn Fairy
awoke and was thrilled to find that the necklace was still safe.
"I'll find a way to give it back today," she said to herself,
"but I must be careful not to be seen."

Later that morning, the Dawn Fairy saw the little girl playing with
her doll in the garden and flew down to hide among the flowers.
"I'll get your coat so you don't get cold," the little girl
told her doll as she ran to the house.

The Dawn Fairy saw her chance, and darting to the doll, she placed the silver necklace around its neck. But just as she did this, the little girl returned. As she stooped to pick up her doll, she blinked and shielded her eyes from a sudden flash of light.

Was the flash of light a reflection from the sun glinting on the sparkling necklace? Or was it really the sunlight on the gleaming wings of the Dawn Fairy as she escaped?
"What a clever doll!" the child cried. "You've found my lost necklace!"